Norman Bates with a Briefcase

The story of Richard Hillman
Soap's best loved villain

**An Unofficial
Coronation Street Companion Book**

By Glenda Young

Published as a paperback in May 2016
by Glenda Young

Cover design by Jo Blakeley

This book is in no way endorsed or authorised by ITV or Coronation Street. It has no official connection to ITV or the television programme Coronation Street.

It is written from the author's personal viewpoint as a Coronation Street fan and as such, may contain errors and omissions.

The characters and situations are fictitious and bear no
resemblance to any persons living or dead.

ISBN-13: 978-1530905041

ISBN-10: 1530905044

All rights reserved.
No part of this publication may be reproduced,
stored in or introduced into a retrieval system, or
transmitted in any form, or by any means (electronic,
mechanical, photocopying, recording or otherwise)
without the prior written permission of the author.

This book is sold subject to the condition that it shall
not, by way of trade or otherwise, be lent, re-sold,
hired out or otherwise circulated without the
author's prior consent in any form of binding or
cover other than that in which it is published and
without a similar condition including this condition
being imposed on the subsequent purchaser.

Dedication

This book is dedicated to all Coronation Street fans
everywhere in the world
from up north to down under
and everywhere else in between

Foreword
by actor Brian Capron
aka Corrie's Richard Hillman

"I never imagined that when I played a humble social worker on Corrie in the 1980a, when I met and worked with iconic actors like Pat Phoenix (Elsie Tanner) Jean Alexander (Hilda Ogden), Peter Adamson (Len Fairclough) and Bernard Youens (Stanley Ogden), that I would return years later to play my part in such an exciting rollercoaster of story that would help Corrie to its first BAFTA.

I still have to pinch myself that I had the good fortune to be cast in the role of Richard Hillman. It was exciting enough to have landed an initial six month contract in Corrie, but to go on such an exhilarating journey with this fabulous storyline, was certainly one the highlights of my acting career.

The superb writers developed an amazing tale that had so many twists and turns on the way to its dramatic denouement and an actor couldn't ask for more challenges than playing this particular complex villain.

Glenda has produced a brilliant account of the rise and fall of Richard.

Reading it brought back so many memories, particularly filming the deaths of Duggie, Richard's first wife Patricia, Maxine and the vain attempts to kill poor old Emily.

Eileen Derbyshire is the sweetest person and we used to laugh and chat together whilst waiting to film a scene and then I'd say, 'Come on Eileen, I've got to try and murder you now!'

None of it would have been possible without the production team and support of the wonderful actors and crew on Corrie, they were like a family to me and I pay tribute to the way Glenda has documented the whole story from beginning to end.

Thank you Glenda, thank you Corrie and thanks to you, the fans throughout the world."

Brian Capron
December 2014

Facts and Figures about…

Coronation Street's Richard Hillman

Richard Hillman is a **fictional character** in **Coronation Street**. He first appeared in the show in June 2001 and last appeared in March 2003.

More than 19.4 million viewers watched on a 2003 spring evening as Richard's reign of terror ended with him driving Gail, David, Sarah-Lou and Bethany into the canal. They lived and Richard died.

More than 15 million people watched Maxine's murder on Coronation Street in January 2003 – causing a surge in demand for power at the end of the episode as they switched on lights and brewed up kettles for a cuppa.

Richard is now rated as one of the best soap villains of all time. He was played by actor **Brian Capron** whose portrayal of Richard Hillman on Coronation Street earned him the following awards and nominations:

Winner
Best Actor in a British Soap - Manchester Evening News Awards

Winner
Best Actor, Best Villain, Best Exit, Best Storyline - British Soap Awards

Winner
Best Villain of the Decade, 2000 – 2010, Inside Soap Awards

Nomination
Best Newcomer - National Television Awards

Nomination
Most Popular Actor - National Television Awards

And if all of that has whetted your appetite, we can now start with the story of Richard Hillman, from his first appearance on Coronation Street to his watery end in the canal… and beyond.

I do hope you're ready for - and that you enjoy – this roller-coaster of a ride with TV soap's best loved villain.

The name's Hillman, Richard Hillman

It's the day of Alma Baldwin's funeral and her friends and loved ones gather outside the church. Following Alma's wishes for her humanist ceremony, the mourners turn up wearing clothes in every colour except black. Audrey Roberts looks lovely in a cream suit and Gail Platt is in lilac. Red is the colour of choice for Emily Bishop, Deirdre Barlow and Vera Duckworth while Janice Battersby goes for the double-denim look.

'Good turn out, isn't it?' says Janice to no-one in particular, as the group waits outside of the church. As the guests gather quietly, waiting to enter the chapel and for the ceremony to start, a tall, dark, handsome stranger appears. He stands at the edge of the group of mourners. Janice is the one who notices him first, standing there all on his own. He clearly hasn't received the request about Alma's wishes for the funeral as he's dressed from head to toe in black. He's very smart though, fitted out nicely in a black suit, a black shirt and a black tie.

'Oh, hello,' says Janice to the man. 'Are you a relative?'
He nods. 'I'm Alma's cousin, Richard.'
Janice introduces Richard to Audrey. 'It's her cousin,' Janice says, as Audrey shakes Richard's hand.
He smiles at Audrey as he gives his full name. 'Richard Hillman.'
'Pleased to meet you,' Audrey says.
'We were quite close as kids, but we lost touch over the years,' says Richard.

'How did you find out she died?' asks Audrey.
'I read it in the paper,' he replies.
Doing the decent thing, as always, Audrey invites Richard back to her house for the buffet after the funeral.

'Oh, I wouldn't want to intrude,' he says, politely. But he accepts Audrey's offer anyway.

Once inside the church, Audrey and Gail pay their respects to Alma. They walk together to stand beside her coffin at the front of the church. The song *Somewhere over the Rainbow* plays quietly in the background as the church fills with Alma's friends.

The mourners fill the church and Richard Hillman takes a seat quietly and without any fuss, at the end of one of the pews.
He sits next to Martin Platt. During the service, Ken Barlow gives a reading in which he rails against the medical profession, blaming it for Alma's death in the mix-up over her cervical smear test. Poor Alma had wrongly been told by her doctor that her smear test result had been normal, when it had in fact shown some cancerous cells. Ken's anger gradually subsides and his sorrow takes over as he ends his reading with the words: 'Alma will always be remembered in our hearts.'

Audrey then stands to read Alma's favourite poem by Mary Elizabeth Frye called *Do not stand at my grave and weep*.

The curtains close against Alma's coffin. The mourners choke back tears as thoughts of Alma fill their hearts and minds. But there's one person in the church who remains unmoved as Audrey reads the poem. Richard Hillman, the man who turned up out of nowhere, shows no emotion at all.

At Audrey's house after the funeral, Richard remains quiet and subdued. He walks around her living-room with a glass of white wine in his hand. He pauses now and then, to listen to other people's conversations. He notes how loved Alma was by eavesdropping on conversations about how much she'll be missed by those present in the room.

Richard takes particular notice of how Alma's death affects those people she loved most and knew best. And so it's words from the likes of Mike Baldwin, Hayley Cropper, Audrey Roberts, Curly Watts and Gail Platt that Richard listens in on, intently.

Janice is impressed with the buffet that Mike Baldwin has laid on. She can't believe that her normally tight-fisted factory boss has paid for all the food for his ex-wife's funeral.

'Baldwin's stumped up for salmon and champagne?' Janice asks, incredulously.

Rita Sullivan replies: 'She meant a lot to him, Janice. She meant a lot to all of us.'

Mike can't eat any of the food he's paid out for, he's too upset over Alma's death, much to the distaste of his new, much younger wife, Linda. 'You have to eat something,' Linda tells him. 'You can't drink on an empty stomach.'

As the guests help themselves to the food, Audrey spies Richard standing on his own. She leads him across the living room to meet her daughter.

'Gail, Gail, have you met Richard?'
'No, I haven't,' she says. Gail smiles at Richard.
'Richard's Alma's cousin,' Audrey tells Gail and then she turns to Richard, 'And this is my daughter, Gail.'
Richard shakes Gail's hand … and holds on to it for just a little too long.
'Pleased to meet you,' she says, smiling again.
The two of them chat politely and Gail asks where Richard has come from.
'Well, I live in Manchester, but my job takes me all over the country.'.
'Oh? What kind of work are you in?'
'I'm a financial advisor,' he says.

After the food, drinks and small talk at the buffet, Audrey asks everyone to be seated. She switches on the TV and Alma's face fills the screen and her voice fills the room. It was one of her last wishes that she could speak to her friends and the people she loved for one final time. In the video, Alma leaves messages for each of them in turn.

She speaks out with messages for Audrey and Gail, for Mike and for Curly, for her friend Hayley who she describes as a 'very special woman'. Those gathered in the room watching the video have tears in their eyes, their grief is too raw to hide.

But there's one person standing at the back of the group, watching all of this unfold before him, with a stony expression on his face. Richard takes in the scene, coldly and calmly, with not an ounce of sorrow showing.

When the wake is over and the mourners leave, Audrey shakes Richard's hand goodbye.

'You must call again,' she tells him.
'I'd like that very much,' he replies.

Richard returns

When Richard reappears into Audrey's life, she's sitting enjoying a drink in The Rovers Return some days later. It's the first time she's seen him since Alma's funeral and while she's somewhat surprised to see him again, she's pleased he's turned up. She talks to him about Alma, whom she's missing a lot, and still grieving for. She finds him charming and extremely polite, very suave and sophisticated. Audrey can tell straight away that Richard is a cut above the Weatherfield men that she usually meets.

She reminisces to Richard about her friend Alma, while Richard listens intently, revealing little of his own past and sharing no memories of his cousin. And then he starts asking Audrey questions about Alma's financial affairs. Audrey puts this down to Richard's professional interest as a financial advisor. She's quite flattered with the attention that Richard is giving her and thinks nothing of Richard's questions about Alma.

In the coming days, Audrey quickly becomes rather taken with Richard. So much so, that she accepts his offer of dinner and Richard takes her out for a lovely meal in a posh restaurant.
This is the sort of date that Audrey loves, it's right up her street. She loves the attention although it does flicker through her mind that Alma had never mentioned her cousin before.

14

When she presses him to talk about Alma, he does know that Alma had been married twice before and he even knows the names of Alma's two ex-husbands – Jim and Mike - so Audrey has no reason to doubt that Richard is who he says he is.

As Audrey and Richard grow closer, Audrey invites him round to dinner at Grasmere Drive. However, their quiet night in is rudely interrupted by Gail who calls round to see her mum, unaware that Audrey is entertaining a gentleman friend. Audrey's annoyed with Gail when she turns up out of the blue and she wants to get rid of her daughter as quickly as she can so she can have Richard all to herself again.

Gail is surprised to find Richard with her mum, but it doesn't take long for her to figure out what's going on. Not wanting to play gooseberry, Gail apologises and leaves Audrey to continue her romantic night in. With Gail out of the way, Audrey continues her seduction of Richard, giving him her best puppy-dog eyes and hanging on to his every word.

Unfortunately for Audrey, Richard's every word is about finance, finance and even more finance. All he wants to talk about are ISAs, investments, savings and bank accounts, particularly Audrey's ISAs, investments, savings and bank accounts. But Audrey is too love-struck to see that Richard might have designs on her purse instead of her heart.

Audrey might not have been too pleased to have Gail turn up and spoil her romantic night in, but Richard was glad of the interruption. He perked up a lot when Gail broke up Audrey's plan for their cosy night in. Audrey didn't notice, but now that Richard has met Gail again, he decides to put a stop to Audrey's amorous intentions.

When Audrey sees Gail next she confides to her daughter that she's sure that Richard's got the hots for her, certain that there's a spark between the two of them. Sadly for Audrey, Richard has already had a quiet, private word with Gail, telling her that he thinks Audrey has fallen for him and that he has no feelings that way for her.

It's left to Gail to break this news to her mum. She tells Audrey that there's no future with Richard. It's news which devastates Audrey and crushes her feelings, but she puts on a brave face and carries on. It's not the first time that Audrey has made a fool of herself over a man, and it certainly won't be the last.

However, while Richard might not have any romantic notions towards Audrey, it's not long before he turns his attentions to Gail.

Love-struck Gail is quickly, too quickly, taken in by Richard, in just the same way as Audrey was before her. Gail immediately warms to Richard's charm and persuasion, his suave sophistication, and it's not long before the two of them start meeting in secret. Gail is too embarrassed to tell her mum that it's her turn to have fallen for Richard now.

Gail's world soon starts to revolve around Richard. So much so that she even forgets Audrey's birthday. Richard takes Gail out for lunch to a cosy country pub and when they return home, they start getting amorous in Gail's living room.

Gail decides to check the answering machine for messages before they head upstairs to bed. And that's when her afternoon love-fest with Richard is cut short by angry messages from Audrey, annoyed at Gail for forgetting her birthday. Instead of leading Richard to bed, Gail does her duty and calls round to see her mum. When Gail arrives at Grasmere Drive, she finds Blanche Hunt is at Audrey's already, paying her birthday respects and hoping for a free drink and some cake. Audrey offers both Gail and Blanche a drink.

'What do you want?' asks Audrey. 'Tea? Coffee?'
'Vodka,' Blanche replies.

Not one for small-talk and subtlety when it's not needed, Blanche soon starts hinting at the availability of Audrey's spare room as somewhere for her to live. On hearing this, Audrey downs the vodka herself to cover her shock at Blanche's heavy hints about moving in. The thought of living with loud-mouth gossip Blanche Hunt is enough to drive anyone to drink.

Gail the Glamorous Granny

As the days and weeks go by, Gail and Richard grow closer and Gail soon starts acting the glamorous granny. Instead of staying in to babysit her granddaughter Bethany when Sarah-Lou goes out, she asks Maxine Peacock to babysit Bethany at her house instead. With the house all to herself, Gail invites Richard round, dims the lights and cooks a romantic dinner. She pulls out all the stops with white wine and a pink tablecloth, candles and small talk. After dinner, she and Richard share coffee, chocolates, cuddles and kisses and then Gail leads Richard upstairs to bed.

Gail's happiness is obvious to everyone. She's in love! She's radiant! At the Rosamund Street medical centre, *MOLLY* Hardcastle the Practice Nurse notices how happy Gail has become. She mentions this to Gail and says she's looking good: 'Dick's put the colour back into your cheeks!'

Gail is certainly happy with the way life with Richard is going and she confides to her friend Sally Webster and her ex-husband Martin Platt about her new love. She readies herself to tell her kids David and Sarah about Richard being the new man in her life.

However, Sarah finds out the news for herself when she bumps into Richard in the house.

And David finds out when he catches his mum in a snog - a full-on snog - with Richard, a man he's never met before in his life! Trust Gail to always go about things the wrong way.

David is upset finding his mum snogging a stranger, and he moves out to live with his dad Martin in his flat. Sarah calls round to see David later that day. She cheers up her brother by suggesting that this Richard bloke, the new man in their mum's life, might just be worth a bob or two. And as he'll be keen to make a good impression on Gail's kids, there could be something in it for the pair of them. Over a family meal later in the Platt house, David apologises to Gail for his reaction to Richard. But he's still clearly troubled over how quickly his mum has taken to the new man in her life. David's upset enough about it that he asks if he can spend the rest of the summer living with Martin at his flat.

With troublesome David out of the family home and living with Martin, Gail and Richard's relationship progresses.

She cooks up a lot of romantic dinners, and tells everyone who'll listen how she's feeling younger, happier and more care-free than she's done in years. She even has her hair cut in a new style (although it doesn't look too different to the old style).

Audrey admires Gail's new hair-do but she's not happy that she went to a fancy hair salon in town instead of having her hair done in *Alma's*.

Audrey has changed the name of her hair salon on Coronation Street to *Alma's* in memory of and in honour of her late friend.

Gail's new lease of life and flattering new hair-do have not gone unnoticed by Richard. He truly seems to be as much in love with Gail as she is in love with him. In fact, he seems too good to be true - although it never passes through Gail's mind that he might not be all that he seems.

Richard is clearly proving a hit with Gail and decides it's time to bond further with Gail's children, particularly David, who can be a bit of a handful at times.

On the night of November 5th, Richard helps David to collect wood to build a bonfire in Gail's back garden.

David gets into the spirit of the event, and he even makes an effigy of a bonfire guy, dressed in an old suit, for burning on the fire. Richard really gets into his surrogate dad role and suggests to David that he buys them some fireworks. You can tell that David has been won over by this idea as he beams back to Richard: 'Thanks, Richie!' instead of his usual, off-hand, cheeky way of addressing him as 'Dick'.

Meanwhile, over in The Rovers, landlord Duggie Ferguson is having trouble with Edna Miller, the pub cleaner.

Edna feels a sense of death and doom around her. She even takes to drinking copious amounts of brandy to quieten the spirits and calm the voices she hears. Or at least that's what she tells Duggie - she could just be after a free drink.

When Duggie asks Edna to tell him what's really bothering her, she tells him in a hushed voice that every pub landlord that she's ever worked for has died while she's been working for them. She feels certain that Duggie will be next!

Duggie doesn't take Edna's words seriously.

Surely, she couldn't be right?

Nosey Norris

Over at No. 3, Emily starts getting wistful about her future. Her thoughts turn to her family and she wonders if she can release some of her hard-earned savings to give to her nephew, Geoffrey - or Spider, as he likes to be called. Emily wants Spider to be able to access his inheritance from her as and when he needs it, and having heard that Gail's new fella is a financial advisor, she wonders if he might be the right person to ask for advice. Emily calls into the medical centre, where Gail works as receptionist. She asks Gail if Richard would mind giving her some financial advice and Gail tells her that her lovely, kind Richard would be only too pleased to help out.

In The Kabin, Emily chats to Rita about her plans to give Spider his inheritance early. Rita warns Emily of the perils of sharing her savings with relatives, after she had a nasty experience with foster daughter Jenny Bradley some years ago. As Rita and Emily chat about money, Richard walks into The Kabin. Emily seizes the moment to make an appointment with Richard to talk through her money options later at home. Of course, he's only too eager to help, as all he sees in Emily is a frail, dotty, little old lady with too much cash on her hands.

At the appointed time Richard calls round to Emily's house, to talk through her financial options. He suggests to Emily that she release the equity in her home and sell it to a company who will guarantee her accommodation in her home, for her lifetime.

Emily is convinced this is the perfect solution, although Norris Cole isn't so sure that either Richard, or Spider, have Emily's best interests at heart. Spider wants to use the money he'll receive from his Aunty Emily's house to set up an organic juice bar in Streatham. When Norris hears about Spider's plans for Emily's money, he intimates nasty, dishonest things about Emily's favourite nephew. Feisty Emily turns on Norris, angrily reminding Norris of the time he found an antique, collectable toy train in the charity box she was filling for the Friends of Weatherfield Hospital. Realising its true worth, Norris tried to cheat Weatherfield Hospital out of receiving the toy train, until Emily put a stop to his dishonesty.

Norris quietens down, he knows when he's out of line, but there's still something bugging him about Richard's financial advice to Emily.

Norris feels the advice Richard is giving Emily isn't quite as sound as it should be, it doesn't have Emily's best interests at heart. He's concerned that Richard is up to no good. But when he tells Emily his suspicions about Richard, she won't hear a bad word said against him and tells Norris to shut up. In The Rovers later, over a drink with Blanche, Emily complains about Norris' behaviour.

Blanche replies acidly: 'You know who he puts me in mind of? Crippen!'

Norris decides to investigate further into the financial agreement that Emily has signed with Richard. He's like a cat who's got the cream when he finds out the shocking news that the director of Kellet Holdings, the company that has bought Emily's house is none other than Richard Hillman himself! And there's more shocking news when Norris discovers that there's a co-director of the company, a woman by the name of Mrs. Patricia Hillman.

How odd, thinks Norris. How very odd indeed.

But when Norris puts these findings to Emily, she's not too concerned. In fact, she's rather put out that Norris has been sticking his nose into her financial affairs. Norris confronts Richard and tells him he knows about the two directors of the company who have bought Emily's house. Richard starts to get irritated with Norris, although he does his best to hide it, and outwardly Richard doesn't seem unduly worried. But he does, immediately, go to see Emily to tell her that she's free to go to a different financial advisor if she chooses.

And then he very casually mentions, as if it must have slipped his mind, that he's a director of the company that would benefit financially from her death.

Oddly, for someone as astute as Emily, this doesn't seem to ring any alarm bells. Richard skips back to see Gail with a huge smile on his face.

Without mentioning Norris' detective work, or being a director of his own finance company, Richard tells Gail that he's got something to tell her. Aware that Norris might rush to Gail with the truth about Kellett Holdings and his co-director being Mrs Hillman, Richard admits to Gail that he hasn't been entirely truthful with her.

Richard had already told Gail that his first wife, Marion, had died but what Gail didn't know was that Richard re-married - to a woman called Patricia. Richard tells Gail that he's divorced from Patricia now, but he fails to mention the finance company arrangement where she's a co-director. Neither does he mention his meeting with Norris and that Norris knows the truth. Richard tells Gail half a story, a truth of sorts, but it's still a bit much for Gail to take in.

Why hadn't he told her before? Why is he telling her now? Richard tells Gail that if she wants to end the relationship, he'll understand. He bows his head, leaves her house, telling her that the ball is in her court. The decision on their future is Gail's to make.

Oh, if only she'd made the right choice back then, none of the following might have happened.

Oh, Gail.

Oh 'eck.

Devious Dicky

It doesn't take long for Gail to make her decision and she phones Richard at home. There's no reply, his phone rings and rings and when she leaves a message on his answerphone, he doesn't call back. Instead, Richard turns up days later at Gail's front door saying he's been working away in the Lake District and hasn't been home.

Gail's overjoyed to see him again and knows she's made the right decision to carry on with their relationship. As they hug each other in the living room, Richard turns his face away from Gail so she can't see his expression. As he hugs her, the sense of relief showing on his face is obvious, but Gail can't see this. Richard knows now how truly gullible Gail is, oblivious to Richard's lies and deceit. She's loved-up again with Richard back in her life. She's ready to forgive, forget and move on. And yes, it's *that* easy for Richard to wheedle his way back into Gail's heart and her life.

It's young David who wonders what's really going on. When he asks Richard why he hadn't returned his mum's calls, Richard tells him that his mobile phone was out of action.

It's clear to David that Richard is lying to Gail. David warns Richard that he's got his eye on him, and that it would be best if he didn't hurt his mum again.

Aware of David's suspicions about him, Richard tries to get back into David's good books and takes him to buy a Christmas tree. On the way there, Emily stops Richard in the street to thank him for the way he's handled her finances. The sale of her house has been finalised and Spider in Streatham is just about ready to open his juice bar.

As Emily and Richard chat on the Street, a man comes looking for Richard, rudely interrupting his conversation with Emily. The man is known to Richard, it's a man by the name of Tony Lawson and he's not a happy man. Tony is the disgruntled son of one of Richard's customers, and he wants a word with Richard, a very strong word indeed.

Tony's mum sold her house to Richard's company, Kellett Holdings, without his knowledge. And Tony is convinced that his mum was coerced into signing his inheritance away and now he's after an explanation from Richard.

It's an explanation that Richard isn't prepared to give, not in front of Emily and he manages to get rid of Tony, for now.

With Richard being harassed by such an unhappy client, he decides to disappear over the Christmas holidays. He knows he needs to go somewhere far, far away and whisks Gail off to see her eldest son Nick in Canada. This leaves David and Sarah celebrating Christmas without their mum and instead they spend the festive season with Martin and Sally.

Audrey isn't best pleased with the arrangements for Christmas as Sally cooks turkey for them all in Gail's kitchen, using an oven she's not familiar with. Martin keeps Audrey merry with sherry in the best way he can. But when Sally brings the turkey out of the oven, it's still not cooked. The sprouts are raw, the pudding is cold and the gas has gone off. It's lucky then, that Roy and Hayley Cropper are cooking up a storm in Roy's Rolls, turning the place into a soup kitchen for the homeless. Norris is helping out and Roy has put him in charge of portion control where he's being very officious: 'It's one can per tramp!'

As the homeless people move on to somewhere more friendly, offering perhaps two cans per tramp, Roy's Rolls is turned over to the residents of Coronation Street who are without gas to cook their dinner. Gail's kids along with Martin and Sally all settle down at Roy's Rolls for a hot Christmas dinner, wearing paper hats they've pulled from crackers.

When Gail and Richard return from their holiday in Canada, they bring presents for the kids and lots of photographs of snow. But as soon as they return home, there's a knock at Gail's door and it's that man again, Tony Lawson. He's still pestering Richard about his mother's house that he felt should have been his. Gail looks on as Richard becomes a little bit nasty and a little bit threatening. He snarls at Tony that if he takes the matter further he'll sue him - and that he'll win.

Proposal

Now then, Audrey has been a woman of independent means since husband Alf died. She's astute with her savings and as she feels she can trust Richard, she invests in a financial portfolio with him. But it comes as some concern when she discovers that her investment is soon down by £6,000. Worried, she confides to Rita in The Kabin and their conversation is overheard by Norris (who overhears everything). Norris tells Audrey the missing money is due to Richard Hillman's wrong doing, as he's a bad 'un and no mistake.

Audrey isn't convinced that Richard is up to no good. She won't hear a bad word said against the man making her daughter so happy. However, Norris won't be swayed and gradually starts putting doubts into Audrey's mind.

With Norris' words ringing in her ears, Audrey is determined to tackle Richard over her missing £6,000 but Richard is equally determined not to be tackled. He reminds Audrey that investments can go down as well as up, and that her savings have gone way, way down.

Ken checks Audrey's investment for her and even he says it looks fine. Reluctantly, Audrey apologises to Richard, but it's become clear that she can't trust him any more and the first seeds of doubt are now planted in her mind.

Gail has now seen the less charming side of Richard. She knows him to be a liar over the Kellett Holdings business. She's seen Richard turn nasty with Tony Lawson and knows there's a dark side to Richard's personality that she didn't know was there when they first met. She also knows that her mum doesn't trust Richard over his dodgy financial advice.

She knows all of this, but she still asks Richard to move in with her to live at No. 8. Richard eagerly accepts Gail's offer and proposes one of his own. He asks Gail to marry him - and she accepts.

Oh Gail, there's no turning back now. If only you had listened to your mother!

Death No. 1 - Duggie Ferguson

Richard makes another proposition, this time of a business kind, asking Duggie Ferguson to go into business with him. Richard wants to redevelop one of the houses he's inherited from his dodgy business dealings and convert it into flats. He knows that Duggie has the contacts and can provide the labour and builders, while Duggie reckons that going into business with Richard will be a way to make some fast cash. Gail warns Richard that Duggie is notorious for cutting quality to keep his costs down, but Richard doesn't listen.

Oh, if only he had!

Richard and Duggie become friendly once they decide to go into business together, and Duggie invites Richard to a game of cards in his flat one night, after The Rovers shuts.

While the card game is in progress, Richard notices Duggie leave the table for a few minutes. He secretly spots Duggie unlock a mini-safe in the living room. From his vantage point at the table, Richard can clearly see that the safe is stuffed with used banknotes.

He thinks it's most likely cash that Duggie's tax man knows nothing about. It's information that Richard keeps to himself and pretends he hasn't seen anything when Duggie returns.

Richard really should have listened to Gail's warning about the poor quality of Duggie's work, though. As the two men work together on the building site converting the house into flats, Richard becomes increasingly concerned about the quality of work from Duggie's men. Duggie shrugs off Richard's concerns, when he confronts him about it.

'What's a few cut corners between friends?' he says.

Later that night, after dark, Richard goes to the house to inspect close-up the work that Duggie's men have been doing. However, unknown to Richard, Duggie finds out where Richard's gone and gets there as quick as he can to stop Richard from seeing too much shoddy work.

But it's too late. Richard is at the house with his torch in his hand and Duggie is there too, in a panic.

The two men are there together in the dark, old, creaky house. They argue over the state of the renovations that have been done so far. Voices are raised and tempers flare.

As they argue, Duggie reaches out to steady himself on the stair banister ... but it's been fitted so badly that the banister pulls away from the wall. Duggie loses his grip and falls two storeys. From his vantage point above Duggie's body, Richard can clearly see that Duggie is still alive. The fall has injured him badly, but he's not dead.

A look flickers across Richard's face as he's not sure whether he should help Duggie, or not. There's a decision Richard must make. Does he call an ambulance or leave Duggie to die? He knows he can't have the cops involved, not Richard, not now. And so he leaves Duggie, badly injured and in pain, lying on the floor, alone.

And then... what does Richard do? Does he ring the police? Does he call out for help? Does he panic? He steals Duggie's keys from his coat pocket and nips straight round to Duggie's flat to steal his stash of cash from the safe.

Then he turns up in The Rovers as cool as you like, just in time for a drink with Gail. With the pub regulars watching, he even rings Duggie's mobile, leaving a message on his voicemail telling him he hopes to speak to him soon.

The next morning, Gail asks Richard if he'll take her to see the house he's been working on with Duggie. He doesn't refuse her request, and confidently expects to see the house swarming with police after Duggie's dead body must have been found. But when Gail and Richard reach the house, there's no-one around. It's deadly quiet. Richard and Gail enter the house and Richard expects to see Duggie's body lying on the floor where he left him after his fall the night before. But there's nothing there! Duggie has gone!

Richard starts to panic.

He walks around the ground floor, flinging open doors and sure enough, in one of the rooms off the hallway, Duggie's body is lying there, motionless. Duggie had dragged himself along the floor, seeking help, after Richard left him the night before. Richard screams and pretends to Gail that he's just 'discovered' the dead body lying on the floor.
Oh dear. It looks like Duggie's cleaner Edna Miller was right after all when she prophesised Duggie's death.

The police are called and news of Duggie's death spreads. Stiff cups of tea are called for in Roy's Rolls.

When news of Duggie's untimely end reaches the staff at The Rovers, barmaid Shelly Unwin sheds a few tears. Eve Elliot calms Shelley with a request using three magic little words across the bar: 'Betty. Brandy. Now!'

Death No. 2 - Patricia Hillman

Once Duggie is buried, Richard breathes a sigh of relief as it looks like he's got away with the perfect crime. He moves in to No. 8 Coronation Street with Gail, David, Sarah and Bethany and acts the perfect family man. He gives Gail his old car and buys a people carrier to ferry his new family around.

But he still needs to find someone to take over as chief builder on the house renovations. Finally, Steve McDonald says he'll do it, on condition that he gets first refusal on one of the new flats at a knocked-down price.

As Richard gets his feet firmly under Gail's table, he spends a day working from home while the kids are off school during half-term. Gail's next-door neighbours are Dr Matt Ramsden and his alcoholic wife Charlie. The Ramsdens are away spending half-term on a skiing trip and they've left their house keys with Gail and Richard. Even the neighbours have come to see Richard as a trusting, family man.

Gail gets butterflies in her stomach when she and Richard pick a wedding date for July.
Life seems idyllic for Gail, she really thinks she's found the man of her dreams. And what a great man he is. Or so Gail thinks.

He gives her friend Sally financial advice when Sally asks Richard to look over her books at the hardware shop.

Sally hasn't realised how deep into debt the shop has gone, until it's too late. Richard's advice to Sally is to re-mortgage her house and invest the cash in the shop. But this is too risky an idea for Sally so she sacks Jason instead to cut down on her costs.

And then Richard proves himself further to Gail by rescuing David and Martin from a fire at Martin's flat. As Richard and Gail are driving past Martin's flat one evening, they see flames shooting from the windows.

Richard leaps out of the car, shoulders the door to Martin's flat, rescues both David and Martin and saves their lives! What a hero! What a man! What a lucky escape for David and Martin.

Can Richard do no wrong?

It seems not, not to Gail any way. When she and Richard get cosy in The Rovers one night, he tells her he sees a rosy future ahead. That is, until Richard's ex-wife Patricia turns up!

Patricia tells Richard she wants to cash in her share of Kellett Holdings, which she reckons is worth about £30,000. After some haggling and arguing, they agree on £25,000 and Richard writes his ex-wife a cheque and waves her out of his life … or so he thinks.

Meanwhile, Jack and Vera Duckworth ask Richard for financial advice.

Richard does his best to put off the Duckworths for as long as he can, assuming they've got no money to spend. Eventually they pin him down to an appointment and set up an investment portfolio with him, or a 'portillo', as Vera mistakenly calls it. Fortunately for Richard - and unlucky for the Duckies - Jack and Vera never expected he would make their money disappear so quickly. Using the Duckworth's £20,000 investment, Richard pays Steve for the building works at the renovated flats.

Despite writing his ex-wife Patricia a cheque, Richard knew it would bounce.
He's not willing to give a penny to her. But Patricia won't be put off that easily. She wants her cash, she wants it now and she's come back to get it.

'Hello Richard,' says Patricia when she turns up at Gail's house with her lips pursed and her arms crossed. 'I think we've got some sorting out to do, don't you?'

Richard pulls Patricia roughly by the arm into the street and away from Gail's door so that Gail can't hear what's going on between them. He tells Patricia he can't pay her because he's got serious money problems and that the renovation has severe subsidence he has to pay for before she gets her share of the cash.

'Does she know I haven't been paid yet?' asks Patricia, nodding towards Gail's house. Then she demands to see if Richard is telling the truth about the renovations.

'I'd quite like to see this subsidence myself.'
'But we're having our tea!' he cries.
Patricia's not put off that easily. 'I want to see it.'
Richard sighs. The only thing he can offer her is proof that he's in deep financial trouble, so he agrees to takes her to see the state of the flats.
'Ok, I'll take you up there later and maybe you'll see sense.'

Richard lies to Gail and tells her he's working late at the office. Instead, he drives Patricia to see the renovation. Patricia isn't impressed by what she sees. All she can make out is a very deep, wide trench in the ground.

'And that's cost forty five thousand quid?' she laughs.
'There's more to do,' says Richard. 'Surveyors to pay for. Structural engineers.'
'I want my money and I'm not leaving till I've got it,' she tells him.
Richard sneers at her. 'Then you've got a long wait.'
'You're not going to swindle me like you do to those old ladies.' she tells him.

Richard pulls Patricia roughly towards him to try to get her to go back to the car.

'Get your hands off me!' she cries. In the fracas, Patricia slips and falls into the gaping hole in the ground. As she scrambles with both feet to try to get a grip on the side of the hole to stop herself falling further, she yells out to Richard.

'I'm going to tell Gail, your clients, every nasty little thing about you. I'll do whatever it takes to ruin you!'
'That really wouldn't be very clever,' snarls Richard.
'I'll go to the authorities, the police. You can kiss goodbye to that nice little family you've got going for yourself. It's all going to end for you, Richard.'

Richard doesn't like what he's hearing, not one little bit. The next thing you know, he picks up a shovel that one of the workmen have left lying around and whacks Patricia over the head with it. It knocks her out stone cold and she falls into the hole below her, her body lying dead at the bottom, in the mud. Richard covers Patricia's body and breathes yet another sigh of relief when the hole – containing Patricia's body - is filled in with concrete at the building site the next day.

He thinks he's safe until Steve finds a silver bangle close to where the concrete has been poured. Richard fobs him off with a lie about the bangle belonging to a woman he's shown around the renovations. Gail finds the bangle in Richard's pocket later as she's sorting things out for dry-cleaning.

And he fobs her off by saying it was a family heirloom that he's picked out for a wedding present to her, that's why he's upset that she's found it. To make amends to Gail and get her on his side again, Richard changes his company details at Kellett Holdings. This new agreement names Gail as his co-director and business partner, instead of Patricia.

Norris kidnapped

Norris is busy volunteering as a steward at the Commonwealth Games but still has time to keep a watchful eye on Emily. When Richard overhears Norris in The Kabin telling Rita that Emily's not feeling well, Richard's ears perk up. He calls straight round to Emily's house, checking out his investment, seeing how close Emily is to death's door, and whether his funds can mature. Fortunately for Emily, she's fine ... this time.

Norris continues to be suspicious, though. He keeps watch over Richard and still doesn't trust him. Richard has had enough of nosey Norris and finally snaps at him in The Kabin.

'I'm going to shut you up once and for all,' Richard sneers.

Norris, in something of a nervous state after Richard's threat, tells him that Rita's upstairs and all he has to do is scream, at which Richard lets Norris go.

Meanwhile, Jack and Vera are still wondering what Richard's got up to with their investment portillo, sorry, their portfolio. They decide to ask Richard to return their savings and this request sends Richard into panic mode. He can't return their cash! He hasn't got it any more!

And so he bamboozles Jack and Vera with gobbledygook and gives them a complicated financial statement that they can't understand.

The Duckies are taken in and Richard's safe again, for now, free to spend what money he does have on buying Nick a ticket to fly in from Canada for his mum's wedding.

Then it's Rita's turn to think about investing her savings with Richard. Norris gives Rita his tuppenceworth as soon as he hears about Rita plans. He tells her that Richard can not and should not be trusted. But it's Rita's own accountant who makes her see that investing with Richard isn't financially sound.
Richard takes the news badly when Rita tells him she won't be investing with him, and he blames Norris for making him miss out on a lucrative bit of business. And then, oh dear, things turn a little spooky for Norris as Richard kidnaps him and threatens to shut him up once and for all.

He bundles Norris into the people carrier and drives him out of town, taking him to the house he's renovating. It's dark. It's quiet. There's no-one around. Richard pushes Norris inside the building. Norris is terrified, too scared to object.

'You've got a narrow mind and a big nose' Richard snarls at Norris. 'It's a lethal combination.'

Norris is terrified that Richard is going to do a Duggie on him and push him down the stairs of doom, but no.

He calmly, very calmly, humiliates Norris.

Richard reels off a few numbers about the money he'll be making when he sells all the flats. So why, Richard asks Norris, does he want to do away with little old Emily, as Norris suspects?

Richard plays his part well, he's serenly terrifying. It's clear that Norris is rattled and scared. And then Richard lets Norris go, after apologising to him with a creepy half-smile.

Gail Potter-Tilsley-Tilsley-Platt-Hillman

It's fair to say that Gail is no stranger to wedding cake. It's also true to say that she's had a complicated history with men. She's already had two husbands – and three marriages - so far in her life at this point.

Her first husband was Brian Tilsley, who she divorced and wed for a second time. When the remarriage to Brian didn't work out, Gail wanted to divorce him again. But Brian died, after being stabbed outside of a nightclub, before their divorce went through. After Brian's death, Gail married Martin Platt, a man much younger than Gail. She divorced Martin when she found out about his affair with a co-worker at the hospital. And now it's time for her to try her luck with husband number three and marry Richard Hillman.

You would think Gail would know what she's doing by now, but alas, it appears not.

It's Gail's hen night in The Rovers, and she's over the moon when Nick walks through the door of the pub, after he flies in all the way from Canada.

On the morning of Gail and Richard's wedding, preparations are in full swing when Richard receives some bad news. The car hire firm have cancelled the limo because his cheque has bounced. Audrey saves the day by arranging for Archie Shuttleworth the undertaker to provide last-minute wedding transport instead.

Richard's best man is an old friend of his called Roger Hinde. Roger is at Gail's house, going over his wedding speech when Richard asks him not to dwell too much on the past in anything he plans to say at the wedding. Clearly, Richard has secrets in his closet he doesn't want revealed.

As with all good weddings, there's something old (Audrey), something new (Nick's new suit), something borrowed (the wedding ring boxes). And something blue turns up in the shape of two policemen knocking at Gail's front door. They demand to know the whereabouts of Richard's ex-wife, Patricia. She'd been expected to arrive in Australia by relatives but as she hasn't turned up there, the cops are making enquiries into her disappearance.

Richard charms his way out of their questions and the two policemen leave. But just when Richard thinks his pre-wedding jitters are over, Roger spots Gail wearing a bracelet he recognises. Roger knows it's the same bracelet that Richard bought for Patricia many years ago.

At the church, the wedding ceremony goes off without a hitch. Richard's speech compares a married couple to a pair of scissors who work perfectly side by side, and woe betide anyone who comes in between them.

After the happy couple swap vows, they head off on honeymoon with Sarah and David to Florida. When they return home to Weatherfield, Gail is carried over the threshold - for the fourth time.

Richard's post-honeymoon blues set in quicker than he would have liked. There's bad news all round when the Hillmans find out that the sale of all four renovated flats have fallen through. Richard's scheme is in danger of being thwarted by a Bail Hostel which is planned to be built next door to the flats. On hearing about the plans for the Bail Hostel, the prospective buyers have bailed out, leaving Richard to start looking for new buyers, all over again. 'I'm ruined,' he cries to Gail.

Richard is in a panic now that his future doesn't look as rosy as he would like. He sweet-talks Councillor Norman (Curly) Watts, thinking he can bribe his way with the council into refusing planning permission for the Hostel. But Curly's not for sale – he never has been nor ever will be.

When Richard moans to Gail about the hole he's found himself in, she jumps right in there with him. 'It's my problem too,' she whimpers, taking her vows of 'for richer, for poorer' a bit too keenly for her own good. Gail suggests re-mortgaging her house and at first Richard isn't keen but he soon comes round. He tells Gail that news about their money problems stay under their roof, she mustn't tell anyone. And he warns her especially to keep this secret from her mum – insisting that Audrey mustn't find out.

He then asks Gail to lie through her teeth so they can get a re-mortgage at the bank under the pretence of a home improvement loan. She does it, even though she makes it clear that she doesn't like doing it. She feels especially bad that she has to hide things from Audrey.

There's a slight reprieve in their finances when Richard sells one of the flats for a knock-down fee of £65,000 but it's clear that the Hillmans are in deep debt right now. Richard even sells his car and pretends it's been stolen, although it gets rather awkward when Gail wonders why he won't claim on the insurance.

Finally, Curly gives Richard some positive news about the Bail Hostel development. The council have received complaints about plans and there will be at least another six months delay before a decision will be made. With that information, along with the money raised from selling his car, and the loan Gail took out on the house, Richard goes back to his bank manager to ask for more cash. But his request is refused.

'What do you want' growls Richard to the bank manager. 'Blood?'
Richard then tells his bank manager that he's got some money coming in to him by the year-end at the latest, from a new source by the name of Mrs. Gail Platt.

Just what is he up to now?

When he arrives home from the bank, Gail - in her dual role as both company director and wife - asks Richard how the meeting with the loans manager went.

'Not bad' says Richard. 'Particularly as I'm expecting a big growth in income over the winter.'

Gail looks a bit confused at this.

'Old people die,' he gently tells her.

Gail is taken aback, but pushes it further with Richard and asks what happens if none of the policies mature.

This sets Richard thinking, and he pops over to The Rovers to find out if one of his policies close to home is close to maturing. He spies Emily at the bar and asks after her health, but he's not too happy with her reply.

'Fit as a fiddle and planning a winter holiday,' says Emily, with a smile.

Disappointed with the news about Emily's health and her policy, Richard then starts to wonder about the size of Audrey's bank account.

Audrey, Archie and arson

With a new son-in-law and a happy daughter, Audrey arranges for a family portrait to be taken. While Audrey and Gail sit down to plan it all out, Richard steals Audrey's house keys from her handbag. He nips down the street, has them copied for himself, and leaves Audrey's set of keys in the hair salon.

When she can't find her keys later Audrey is confused and extremely upset. She enlists David to help her retrace her steps to see if she can remember when she last had them. David finds them in the salon and poor Audrey blames herself for losing her keys. She can't understand it as she's never done anything like this before.

The portrait photographer arrives at Gail's house. Although they've had enough notice and she's laid out a clean outfit for David, Gail decides that the clothes she wears to clean the house in are good enough to be preserved in perpetuity. Sarah is sulking that having to stay in the house because of the photographer is stopping her from going out with her boyfriend Aidan Critchley.

The photograph is taken, with Richard firmly and squarely pictured at the front and centre of his new family. After the photographer leaves, Richard takes Audrey's house keys again.

He lets himself into her house on Grasmere Drive, doing nothing more than turning the radio on before he leaves. When she returns home, Audrey is convinced she's starting to go a little mad. First, it was losing her keys and now she's leaving the radio playing in an empty house? Audrey's confusion is all going perfectly according to Richard's plan. He intends to drive Audrey round the bend, to think she's got dementia, and then collect on her inheritance. That way he gets rid of Gail's interfering mum while at the same time he cashes in to clear his debts.

Now that Richard has a spare set of keys to Audrey's, he pops there again while she's out and turns off her burglar alarm. He wanders around and decides to leave the stereo on before he locks up and leaves. When Audrey arrives home later, with David by her side, they hear 'voices' coming from the living room. David laughs at his gran for leaving the stereo on, but she feels certain that she switched the stereo off.

Poor Audrey.

Richard pays Audrey's house another little visit. But what he doesn't know, this time, is that Gail and Audrey are on their way there as Audrey has left work early with a migraine. With Richard already in Audrey's house snooping around, he hears Gail and Audrey enter. Audrey finds the alarm switched off again, she can't believe it as she was sure that she'd set it.

49

Richard hears Audrey and Gail coming into the house and he hides in the larder. It's the same larder where Audrey keeps her biscuits ... the same biscuits that she wants with the cup of tea Gail is making for her! In the larder, Richard panics. Luckily for Richard, Audrey remembers just in the nick of time that the biscuits aren't in the larder after all, they're in the kitchen cupboard.

As Gail and Audrey drink their tea and eat their biscuits, Gail decides to phone Richard on his mobile to let him know she'll be late home. Richard has left his phone in Audrey's kitchen and as Gail is dialling his number, he quietly leaves the larder and switches off the phone before it starts to ring and give his game away.

It's another narrow escape for Richard.

But Richard's lies soon start to close in on him. After he sold his people carrier, and lied to everyone that it had been stolen, he's shocked when Audrey tells him that she's found his car, for sale in a garage in town. After insisting the car she saw actually was his, Audrey demands to accompany Gail and Richard to the car lot. She's having doubts about Richard's behaviour and wants to know what's going on

At the garage, Richard tells Gail and Audrey to wait outside while he talks to the salesman. It's the same salesman who bought the car from him. Richard makes an excuse about wanting to buy something, just so it looks to Gail and Audrey, from a distance, that he's being shown proof of purchase. Back in the car, Richard lies that the salesman had shown him a receipt for the car that he had bought from someone else. He covers his lies by telling Audrey it's definitely not the same car as the one he had stolen. Audrey knows it's the same car, she knows she's right, and the little doubts she started having about Richard soon start to grow into much bigger ones.

A card arrives in the mail to announce that the family portrait photograph is ready to collect. Sarah sniffs that they had better get it quickly as it will be the last photo they have of David without a prison number underneath his mug shot. Richard suggests inviting Audrey round to have a look at the picture. Gail manages to catch her on the phone just as Audrey is setting her washing machine going. When Audrey arrives at Gail's, Richard slips over to Audrey's to cause more mischief. When she returns home she finds all of her washing hung out to dry. How odd, she thinks. She later confides to Rita and Archie that she thinks she's starting to have 'senior moments'.

Over at Gail's house, there's a knock at the door. It's the police. Again. They want to talk to Richard about his ex-wife Patricia. Again. A body has been found and they believe it to be her. Gail tries to reassure Richard that it may not be Patricia.

'Oh, it will be,' he mutters, darkly.

Richard goes to the morgue to identify the body. It's not Patricia, of course.

While she should have been down under in Australia, her body is instead down under the concrete foundations of the renovated flats. Richard lies to Gail and says it is Patricia's body, and that he thinks Patricia must have committed suicide.

Fortunately for Richard the police call round just in the nick of time to say there's been a mix up. After Richard identified Patricia's body, the dental records have been checked which prove it's not Patricia's body after all.

When Norris gets wind of a dead ex-wife of Tricky Dicky, as he's now started calling Richard, he's absolutely convinced that something isn't right with Richard. Richard asks Archie to arrange the cremation - as soon as possible, too. However, Patricia's friend Charlotte flies in from Australia. She wants to identify her friend's body at the morgue and although Richard does all her can to dissuade her from doing so, she's adamant she'll do it, to say goodbye to her friend.

Gail does her best to be hospitable to Charlotte and invites her to stay for dinner, although as you can imagine, Richard isn't keen to have her hanging around for fear of her asking dodgy questions.

But she does stay, and Charlotte spots Patricia's bracelet on Gail's arm. She knows straight away that it's the bracelet that belonged to Patricia, a favourite one that she loved. Richard once again manages to squirm his way out of the awkwardness. This time he says it was his grandmother's bracelet that Patricia wore, as his wife, and now Gail is wearing it, as his wife. At the end of a very awkward dinner, Richard drives Charlotte home. He threatens her in the car, in a quietly menacing way, by the light of his dashboard and returns home to Gail.

'I think that's the last we'll see of Charlotte,' he says, with menace in his eyes.

Sarah in a coma

Policewoman Emma Watts, Curly's wife, knocks at Gail's door.

'It's bad news, I'm afraid' she says.
'Patricia?' asks Richard, in a panic.
'Sarah?' whispers Gail.

Sadly for Gail, the bad news is about Sarah. She's been badly injured in a car crash. Aidan Critchley had stolen Ken's car and with Sarah in the passenger seat, took the car joyriding around Weatherfield. Aidan gathered speed and ultimately lost control of the car. As Sarah tried to leap out of the moving car, it overturned and smashed into the back of a wagon. Aidan did a runner, leaving Sarah lying bleeding under the wreckage. A passer-by called the police as Aidan ran away from the scene.

And so Gail rushes to hospital where Sarah's having brain surgery and there's every possibility that she might not make it. Sarah is in a coma, Gail is in a state, Candice is in tears and David cries a heartfelt plea to his sister for her to get better soon.

Fortunately, Sarah recovers. And slowly but surely the memory of what happened comes flooding back to her. After she makes a statement to the police, Aidan is arrested at Weatherfield Comprehensive School and accompanied to the station by the cops.

At the school, Ken breathes a sigh of relief that Aidan's behind bars.

Everyone is horrified to hear Aidan left Sarah to die. So Ken can't believe his eyes when later that same day Aidan turns up at school and returns to the classroom where Ken is teaching. Aidan winds Ken up and taunts him about being a 1960s liberal, the likes of which allowed leniency in the law in the treatment of juveniles - laws which have released him on bail and out of jail.

Back home at Gail's house, Richard and Gail argue about being deep in debt and then, suddenly, Richard turns the whole thing around. He blames himself for Sarah's accident, and for the family's finances falling apart. And what does Gail do? She cuddles his head to her bosom and tells him she loves him.

What an evil bloke!

What a stupid woman!

Audrey, still confused and upset and certain she's losing her mind, has the locks changed on her house. This foils Richard's plans to get into her house and move things around, that is - until she trusts Gail and Richard with a spare set of new keys. Richard returns to Audrey's house one night while she's sleeping, determined to put an end to her once and for all, and cash in on her savings. He takes the battery out of Audrey's smoke alarm and sets fire to her house.

As Audrey sleeps soundly upstairs in bed, the fire takes hold in the living room downstairs.

It's not long before the flames rage and smoke drifts upstairs. Audrey wakes, coughing against the smoke. She gets up out of bed in a right state, and falls, knocking herself unconscious, as the fire rages on.

Just then, Archie and Steve pull up outside of Audrey's house. They see the flames shooting from her windows, and immediately spring into action. Steve smashes the front door down and breaks windows to get into the house, before dialing 999.

'Audrey! Audrey!' yells Steve as he dashes into her house through the smoke.

He finds Audrey's body lying at the bottom of the stairs and drags her outside, away from the fire and smoke, just as the fire brigade arrive.

While all of this drama is going on at Audrey's house, Gail is fast asleep in bed at home. Lying beside her in bed is Richard, wide awake, wondering if his plan has worked and Audrey is dead.

There's a knock at Gail's door in the middle of the night. It's Archie.

'It's Audrey! There's been a fire! At her house!'
'Is she dead?' cries Gail.

It's a question that Richard is very interested in hearing the answer to.

'No, not dead,' says Archie. 'She's at Weatherfield General.'

Gail rushes upstairs to get dressed and Richard takes Archie to one side to quiz him further about Audrey's condition.

'Ok. How bad is she?' says Richard, demanding an immediate reply.

'Like I said, she's unconscious. She didn't look good, there was a lot of smoke.'

But Richard wants to know more.

'What do you reckon?'
'Well, it's the smoke that kills,' says Archie, looking worried.

Gail and Richard rush to Weatherfield General where Audrey's been taken into intensive care. Richard asks the doctor how Audrey managed to survive the flames and all of the smoke.

He says: 'It turns out that she was unconscious, and she fell. From the bruising on her head it looks as if she must have got out of bed and fallen downstairs. This put her below the level of the worst fumes.'

The doctor turns to Richard and says: 'She's a very lucky woman'

Richard sneers, and replies: 'Isn't she just?'

When Audrey recovers and returns home from hospital, Richard tells anyone who'll listen that Audrey is a danger to herself. He tries to poison the minds of everyone who knows Audrey so that they'll see her as a dotty old woman, unsafe to be left on her own.

But Audrey has finally worked out what has happened with the fire. Her earlier doubts about Richard mean that she's been putting two and two together and realises now that Richard is behind it all. Her confused state of mind, leaving the radio on in the house, losing her keys, his car he said had been stolen but she saw in the garage, it all adds up and Audrey knows that Richard is behind the fire too. She's not the daft old lady that Richard would like everyone to think she is. Audrey is far more astute than that and she knows now, for sure, that Richard isn't what he seems.

Audrey plans to go back to work, unaware that Richard has decided she's not safe to be left on her own. When she hears Gail and Richard discussing how to get Power of Attorney over her affairs, it's too much for her to bear. Audrey storms out of Gail's house and in a panic to get away from Richard as quickly as she can, she runs off.

Richard gives chase as Audrey runs all the way along the canal path until she reaches Archie's house where she begs to be let in. Richard follows her and with Audrey now inside Archie's house, Richard bangs on the front door demanding to be let in too.

'He's trying to kill me,' cries Audrey to a shocked Archie. 'He wants my money!'

Audrey turns hysterical as Richard tries to force his way into the house and she screams at Archie to get Richard out of the house.

'She's not well,' Richard calmly tells Archie. 'She's just confused. It's been coming on for quite a while.'

Archie politely but firmly shoves Richard out of the door. He tells him to leave and go home.

'I heard him talking about my will, about Power of Attorney,' Audrey tells Archie. 'He'll get my money when I die!'
'You're not going to die,' says Archie.
'That's what he wants!'
Archie doesn't believe Audrey at first as she confides in him about Richard's plan of evil over the last few months.

'I'm not mistaken, I'm not confused,' she tells Archie. 'He's trying to kill me! Archie, please. If you don't believe me, no-one will.'

Audrey finally makes Archie see the truth about Richard. To Audrey's relief, Norris also tells her that he believes her every word.

With Archie by her side, Audrey tells her tale to the police and Richard is called in for questioning.

But he easily punches holes in Audrey's story when he reveals that Audrey has an appointment with the specialist at the hospital to test for senile dementia.

Even though it's an appointment that Audrey has made for herself, to prove to herself that she's not going mad, the police take their questions no further.

Knowing her family is no longer safe living under the same roof as Richard, Audrey tries to kidnap Sarah and David, which deteriorates her relationship with Gail still further.

Archie advises Audrey to see a solicitor to change her will, which she does. She tells Richard there's no point in bumping her off now as he won't get a penny from her will.

Gail thinks her mother's gone bonkers and tells her never to darken her doorstep again. It's too much for Gail to take in. She's still on Richard's side and believes her new husband can simply do no wrong.

The end of Emily?

It's now almost Christmas and Richard isn't happy with the NHS for giving out free flu-jabs to pensioners. He's still waiting for some of his old ladies to die during the winter, and for his policies to mature. The free flu-jabs are a nuisance to his plans as they're keeping his old ladies alive much longer than he'd like. He decides to check up on Emily's health again, feigning concern as he's heard she's not well.

Emily is tired when he calls round. She offers Richard a glass of sherry but soon starts feeling sleepy in her chair after they've had a little chat. Richard takes the sherry glass from Emily's hand.

'Would you like me to help you upstairs, perhaps?' he offers. Emily shakes her head, no.

'I've got things to do. How are you and Gail and the family?' she asks, sleepily.

'Very well,' Richard replies. 'Although Audrey's got some silly ideas in her head just at the moment.'

'I've been very grateful for your financial help,' Emily tells him. 'Although, as I understand it, you don't really make anything out of it until after my death, do you?'

'Not really, no,' he says.

Emily yawns and struggles to stay awake.

'You just rest, just relax. I'll finish my drink and let myself out,' Richard says as Emily closes her eyes and falls asleep. He waits until he's sure that Emily is properly asleep and then he leans over her body.

'Emily? Are you asleep?' he whispers into her ear.

There's no response from Emily. Richard picks up a cushion from her chair and puts it to Emily's face, ready to suffocate her. But he can't do it, he just can't do it and he pulls the cushion back. He steels himself and is just about to try again with the cushion when Rita walks into Emily's house, without knocking first.

Richard jumps with shock.

'Hello Rita, I just called in,' he says. Rita gives him an odd look. She's more than a little surprised to see Richard there with Emily.

Emily wakes up when she hears Rita's voice.

'How are you feeling Emily?' asks Rita.

'Tired,' says Emily. 'But… surviving.'

Richard heads back home to Gail and tells her: 'I just stopped off at Emily's. To tell you the truth Gail, I don't think she's long for this world.'

Death No. 3 – Maxine Peacock

Richard's money problems continue to worry both him and his bank manager. He's called in, yet again, to explain himself at the bank. The bank manager tells Richard that he's got until the end of the year before bankruptcy charges are filed, and tells Richard: 'So… I hope you make a killing!'

Oh, if only he knew.

Richard knows the only way he can get out of trouble with the bank and pay off his debts is if he can cash in one of his old ladies' policies. He decides it's time for Emily's policy to mature, which can only mean one thing, and it doesn't bode well for poor Mrs. Bishop.

Over at The Rovers, there's a party to celebrate. Maxine's mum Doreen's 50th birthday. There's also a celebration for Todd Grimshaw's 18th at the same time and the pub is in full swing with party-goers.

Emily is babysitting little Josh for Ashley and Maxine and Richard sees this as his chance to do in Emily while everyone's drunk and having fun in the pub.
But before he sets off to kill Emily, Richard plans in advance. Now that Richard knows Aidan is living rough in the hardware shop, he wants to make it appear as if Aidan is the one who has attacked Emily. First, he takes some of Audrey's sedatives and puts them into a bottle of booze.

He leaves the booze along with some food for Aidan, who drinks it all down and eats all the food, believing it's been left for him by Sarah who has been supplying him with his only source of food while he's been living rough.

Then, with Aidan knocked out by the drugs and the booze, Richard takes Aidan's coat, baseball hat and trainers to wear. He picks up a crow bar and crosses the street, dressed as Aidan. Richard climbs over the wall at the back of the Peacocks' house and sneaks into the kitchen from the back yard.

As Emily watches an old film on TV, she doesn't hear or see Richard enter the house. The kitchen door is behind her, and she's engrossed in the film. Richard creeps up behind Emily as she sits on the sofa and without pausing, he brings the crow bar crashing down on her head.

He thinks he's done it, he thinks he's killed Emily stone cold dead. Just at that very moment, Maxine enters the house through the front door. She's left the pub to check up on baby Josh. She's alarmed when she sees Richard standing in her living room with the crow bar in her hand, and Emily slumped on the sofa.

'Richard? What are you doing?' she stutters.

Richard eyes her, coldly. 'You should have stayed at the party, Maxine.'

Baby Josh's cries can be heard coming from his bedroom upstairs. Maxine lifts her eyes in the direction of her baby's voice. In that split second, Richard lunges forward, and brings the crow bar crashing down on Maxine's head. She falls to the floor, dead.

Richard throws DVDs and CDs into a bag, to make it look as if there's been a burglary in the house, before disappearing back through the kitchen door and into the garden. He takes the bag of stolen goods and leaves it beside Aidan's sleeping body along with Aidan's clothes he removes and places beside Aidan. After cleaning himself up, Richard heads to The Rovers and joins in the celebrations for Maxine's mum's birthday. He insists on buying Ashley a drink, to keep him in the pub instead of returning home to find Maxine's dead body.

'Lovely couple!' says Gail, about Ashley and Maxine.
'Aren't they just?' replies Richard, smiling.

Ashley finally returns home. 'I'm back,' he shouts as he enters the house. 'I couldn't flaming get away…'.
Then he stops, shocked to find two bodies in his living room. Maxine is sprawled on the floor, and Emily is slumped on the sofa. He can't believe what he's seeing and stands open-mouthed, in shock and fear. Just at that moment, Norris knocks at the front door, he's calling to escort Emily home from babysitting duties, but he ends up ringing the police when he finds Ashley - and the bodies.

Fortunately, Emily survives the attack. 'She's alive! Emily!' cries Norris. But Maxine, however, is most definitely dead. By the time the police and the ambulances arrive, Richard is still drinking in The Rovers, enjoying another half pint of beer and showing no sign of remorse.

Ashley is taken in for questioning and kept in the cells, unable to talk to anyone until he's eliminated from police enquiries. Doreen's in distress and Ashley's in shock for days. He can't even bring himself to talk about arranging Maxine's funeral until Archie Shuttleworth subtly makes him see sense.

Just as Richard has planned, Aidan is arrested for Maxine's murder and for the attack on Emily. Aidan knows he'll need help to get him out of being framed for a murder he didn't commit. He calls on the one person he knows he can trust – his teacher Mr Barlow from school. Ken is reluctant at first but he knows what Aidan is capable of and what he isn't and he believes in Aidan's innocence, which is more than some of Ken's neighbours do.

Meanwhile, back at the hospital, Emily makes a slow, but full recovery.

'Glory! Glory!' cries Norris.

Richard has trouble coming to terms with what he's done. He's not sleeping, he goes wandering around the house, unable to rest.

He twitches Gail's net curtains when he peers through the windows to see what's happening outside. When he receives a phone call to say that one of his investments has paid up £23,000 after one of his old ladies dies, he can't believe the irony of it. There was no point in trying to kill Emily after all.

Maxine's funeral

With Archie's help, Ashley organises Maxine's funeral. In the church, Fred Elliott stands to give a reading and then Maxine's dad Derek tries to follow, but he breaks down on the pulpit, in tears. Fred helps him back to his pew then turns to see who is sitting behind him. He spies Richard and asks him to take over with Derek's speech.

'You couldn't do the honours, could you?' whispers Fred to Richard.
'Who? Me?'
'There's none of us can do it and you're nearest.'
'There must be somebody here who knew her better than I did,' he pleads.

Gail encourages Richard to continue with the reading.
'It doesn't matter, Richard. Everybody's waiting,' she says.

Richard is clearly uncomfortable about this, but feels he can't refuse. He stands and walks to the front of the church to continue with the reading. Audrey and Norris are stunned to see Richard take over the reading.

'I'd like to share a few thoughts of my own with you about Maxine,' Richard says. 'The truth is … I have a confession to make.'

A confession?

Audrey's face is a picture, she can't believe what Richard has just said.

Richard continues: 'What happened to Maxine, it shouldn't have happened. It wasn't intended. A lovely young woman taken away, that can't be right. So I confess ... I confess that ... when I heard what had happened I stopped believing there could be any good in this world. You could say I've lost all faith.'

Outside, at the graveside, it's too much for Audrey to bear when she sees Richard take Gail's hand. She's convinced Richard is the one who murdered Maxine and who tried to kill Emily. And she's right too, but not everyone else feels the same.

'It's you what did it!' she screams 'It's you, Richard! You killed her! You killed her like you tried to kill me and you were going to kill Emily. Admit it, go on. You were going to do it earlier. He was! Now he's mocking all of us.'

Fred quietens Audrey: 'Can we remember the nature of the occasion and show some respect?'

Archie also tries to calm Audrey and later in The Rovers, Audrey apologies to Ashley who is clearly angry with her for her outburst at Maxine's grave. Richard comes out of all of this smelling of roses, the hero of the hour for standing in at the church and doing the reading. Maxine's parents insist he join them for a drink.

In the pub, Norris and Audrey chat quietly together. They know they've got to do something about Richard, but what?

Richard's confession

There's good news for Richard when he finds out the Bail Hostel isn't going to be built. He's overwhelmed, overjoyed and suggests to Gail that they buy a new house far away from Coronation Street. But as all of this is going on and Richard is buzzing with good news and plans for the future, Aidan rings Sarah from the young offender's institution where he's been placed on the wrongful charge of Maxine's murder. He tells Sarah he needs to speak to her urgently about something important.

Sarah visits Aidan and he tells her that he's received the results of his blood test from the night of Maxine's murder. After Richard doped him up with Audrey's sedatives, the police reckon that there's no way Aidan could have carried out the murder as there were enough pills in his system to knock out a large horse, never mind a teenage boy.

Sarah takes this news back to Audrey who insists she tell her mum straight away. But like any other teenager who's told to do something she should, she doesn't.

And so it's left to Audrey to break the news to Gail that Aidan couldn't have been the killer. She also asks Gail if she knows where her sedatives disappeared to that she'd left at Gail's house.

Slowly, slowly, pieces of a puzzle start to join up and make sense and the truth gradually, finally, dawns on gullible Gail. Two and two start adding up to four in Gail's head, and she knows, oh yes she knows, that the man she loves is the man who murdered Maxine. As the realisation sinks in, Gail's mouth takes on the shape it would make if it had got stuck on the *lo* part of the word *baloney*.

Gail knows she has no choice but to confront Richard with what she's been told.

'You had my mum's pills. I saw you with them on the night Maxine was murdered,' she says.
'What's this, Gail? What's bothering you?' asks Richard, startled.
'I'm wondering about things that have happened. All the trouble with my mum.'
'Ah! She's been putting poison in about me, has she?' he spits.
'Not just that. I saw the way you looked at Ashley tonight. Like you were seeing terrible things.'
Richard starts to wonder where this is going. 'Oh come on, Gail.'
'I have to know, Richard. I can't stand what I'm starting to think. Please, tell me the truth.
'I always tell you the truth, Gail,' he lies.
'You didn't kill Maxine, did you?'

Richard stays silent and stares at Gail. She knows the answer to that question already.
 'I won't lie to you, Gail. Perhaps this is all for the best. Yes, it was me. I just want you to understand ... it was an accident'

'An accident!' Gail screams, incredulously. 'How could it have been an accident? She was hit over the head with a crow bar!'
'She wasn't supposed to be there.'
It slowly dawns on Gail what Richard had planned to happen.
'It was supposed to be Emily you were after?'
'No,' he lies again.
'My mum was right all along.'
'I wanted to get back at Aidan, the scumbag who almost killed our daughter, I wanted to get rid of him. I've done a terrible thing. I know that and you have every right to be angry. Please before you do anything else, let me tell you what happened, OK?'

Richard holds Gail's arms tightly and she calms down enough to listen to what he has to say. He confesses about taking Aidan's trainers and clothes to frame him for Maxine's murder.

'I never meant to kill anyone,' he says. 'You've got to believe me. I just meant to stage a robbery to get Aidan out of our Sarah's life once and for all. When he left our Sarah at death's door in the hospital you would have done anything to have Aidan Critchley rot in hell, wouldn't you?'
'Yes,' nods Gail. 'But …'
'It was an accident. I swear. I panicked. I lashed out. I couldn't understand why she was attracted to scum like him.'

'She gets it off her mother,' says Gail coldly. 'Archie, Norris, they were right about you all along. They knew what you were up to and I was too stupid to see what was going on. Old people died, we inherited their property and I thought nothing of it. We've got a brand new car, a big new house and it's all been paid for with blood money.'

Terrified and in a panic, Gail tries to run and leave the house but Richard grabs her and holds her back.

'Gail, I'm sorry. I'm really sorry. It's been a nightmare. If only I could turn back the clock but I can't.'
Richard starts crying. 'Those flats were cursed from day one.'
'Duggie?' asks Gail. 'Did you kill Duggie?'
'All my problems go back to him. He fell. I swear on our kids' lives. I didn't kill him.'
'What about Patricia? Did you kill her?'
'Yes.' he confesses.
'Oh God!' cries Gail.
'Oh Gail!' cries Richard. 'Everything I've done, I've done for you. I've killed for you, Gail. Did Martin or Brian love you that much? They didn't love you enough to stay with you! If you lived for a thousand years you'll never find anyone who loves you as much as I do.'
Gail can't believe what she's hearing.

Richard continues. 'It's like that quote from our wedding speech, about a married couple being like a pair of scissors, working together. We're joined so we can be separate, sometimes moving in different directions. But woe betide anyone who gets between us.'

He pauses and looks at Gail, begging her to believe him. Richard hands Gail the advertising brochure for their new, big house they were planning to move into.

'Some people threatened our future. I had to get rid of them. But what's done is done. I've got all I needed. You and me will be so special. We'll leave this tatty street behind and live happily ever after.'

Gail looks at the house brochure in her hand.

'I'll put the kettle on,' Richard says, as if it's a normal thing to do under the circumstances. Gail isn't taken in by his calmness and rips up the brochure, yelling at Richard: 'Why should I believe you? You tried to kill my mother! I'm going to ring the police'.

Gail lunges at the telephone but Richard gets there before her, yanks the phone out of the wall socket and the phone falls to the floor.

'You're not just evil, you're sick!' Gail yells at him.
'I just put my family first, Gail. Animal instincts, looking after our kids,' he replies, coolly.
'They're not *your* kids!' Gail screams.

Richard is hurt by this, he's clearly taken aback by Gail's words.

'I like to think of them as mine,' he says quietly.

'It's not me you love,' says Gail. 'It never has been. It's the ready-made family - because you can't make one of your own.'

'I love you,' he cries to Gail.

Gail whispers back to him. 'I hate you.' and then louder, much louder, building to a scream, she repeats her words.

'I HATE YOU!'

'Where is Patricia?' Gail asks. 'Where is she? How many people died because of those flats? Tell me the truth, Richard! Did you kill her?'

'Yes,' he admits. 'Gail, she was a vicious, spiteful cow. She hated to see me with the family I'd always wanted. She wanted half of Kellett Holdings. We had the wedding coming up, the honeymoon. I was under a lot of pressure. She threatened our whole future, I had to stop her.'

'What did you do?'

'I hit her with a spade. She's buried in the foundations of the flats. That's how Steve McDonald found her bracelet. It must have slipped off during our struggle. It was heat of the moment stuff, done in anger. But I killed her, there's no getting away from that. And killing her made it easier to think about killing again. I know I scared you just now but you can trust me, I swear. No need for any more lies, I'll always be there for you.'

'Oh yeah,' laughs Gail. 'You'll never have a seedy little affair but you might hit me in the face with a shovel!'

'No, never.'
'You think that running off with another woman is a worse crime that clubbing someone to death. You're twisted. You're Norman Bates with a briefcase and I don't want you living under the same roof as my family. It's over.'

Oh. Gail, if only it was!

Duckworth dosh

After confessing his catalogue of crimes and grisly murders to Gail, Richard runs out into the night and disappears. Gail tells the police everything and news spreads around Weatherfield and further afield. Journalists turn up wanting grisly details about Richard Hillman, the murderer. Gail is left alone in shock and in tears. Of course Norris wastes no time in swapping notes with the journalists and photographers who set up camp in Gail's front garden and who torment the neighbours for quotes and juicy gossip about Killer Hillman.

Worried for the kids and concerned for his ex-wife, Martin moves back in with Gail temporarily when he finds out that Gail has started drinking to cope. She hits the bottle hard in an attempt to get to grips with the reality of life with Richard Hillman. Yet, despite everything that has happened, Gail still maintains her love for Richard and tries to cope with the fact that her fella was a psycho. The police unearth Patricia's body at the flats and although Audrey deserves an apology from the police about being right about Richard all along, she doesn't get one.
Blanche comments about the neighbours: 'There's folk round here with humble pie to eat.'

Meanwhile, Jack and Vera wonder what has become of their money they gave to Richard to invest. When Jack calls the number of the company Richard is supposed to have invested their deposit with, the line is dead.

Ken checks out the firm's name for them but finds nothing. Richard has covered his tracks too well. The Duckworths decide to fight for their cash and are furious with Gail, blaming her for the loss of their savings. Vera is so incensed by what's happened that she chucks a brick through Gail's window. The next morning over breakfast, Vera and Jack chat about their missing cash.

'Do you know, I never slept a wink last night,' says Vera, at the breakfast table.
Jack nods in agreement. 'Me neither. I kept expecting the police knocking on the door.'
'Well, I don't give a monkey's if they do. All I worry about is me and you and we *need* that money!'
'We've been skint most of our lives, so what's so special about now?' asks Jack.
'We can't afford to kiss twenty thousand pounds goodbye.'
'I am just as upset as you about losing that money.'
'No you're not. You're not nearly as upset as me.'
'Vera …' Jack tries to calm her. 'We've got us pensions. We've got us lodging money off young Tyrone. You've got your little part-time job. We're not going to flaming starve, are we?'
'Look, I am not working myself into an early grave!' Vera shouts, banging the table with her fist. 'I want every penny of that money back.'
'You heard what Gail said. It makes no odds what you do, the money has gone.'
'She's not going to get away with this.'

'Vera ... she nearly lost her life. And her kids. And she's likely going to lose that house. So how much suffering has she got to go through before you leave her be?'
'I'll leave her be when she pays us back what she owes us.'

Jack sighs. He knows Vera won't be stopped and she takes her opportunity to get one over on Gail when she meets a journalist sniffing around for a story on Richard. Vera sells her story, and her friendship with Gail, to the papers for £500. She lays the blame for Richard Hillman's actions squarely with Gail.

Vera tells the press: 'They were married, she must have known what was going on. Married people don't have secrets.'

Jack just rolls his eyes.

Someone else who goes to see Gail after the news breaks about Richard is Ashley. He's confused, hurt and angry and blames Gail for the death of his wife. Despite being attacked by the neighbours and people she once thought as friends, Gail starts doing her best to pull herself out of the doldrums, to stop drinking and get back on with her life. With support from Martin and Audrey, she makes a new start and goes to see her solicitor.

But just when things look like they might be getting better for Gail, two weeks after Richard's disappearance, a dark shadow appears on the cobbles.

Richard returns

The dark shadow on the cobbles is a Richard-sized shadow. He enters Gail's house when he knows it's empty and waits for David to return from school. When he does, Richard grabs him. Then Sarah returns home from seeing Todd and Richard grabs her, with little Bethany too. And then Gail returns home, horrified, terrified to see Richard back, there in her home.

'What have you done to the children?' she screams at Richard. He stands calmly and quietly in Gail's living room, dressed in his wedding suit and tie.

'There's nothing to be afraid of, Gail,' he hisses. 'Keep calm and you won't get hurt.'

But keeping calm is something that Gail isn't prepared to do. She struggles with Richard and he tries to pin her down to the floor. He puts his hand across her mouth to stop her from screaming. Gail bites his fingers, but it's not enough to stop him from continuing.

'If you want to see Sarah and David and little Bethany then you have to keep quiet. Do you understand, Gail? Don't scream. I don't want to hurt you or the kids. I just want you to listen to what I have to say.'
'Where are they?' demands Gail. 'Where are the children?'
'They're safe,' is all Richard will say.
'What do you want, Richard?'

'I've seen the papers. I've seen what they're saying about you. I've come back to make amends. I've written a confession, it'll totally clear your name, it'll vindicate you.'

'You should hand yourself in Richard. Get a good lawyer.' Gail is desperate now, grasping at straws to say the right thing, anything to get Richard to stop what he's doing.

'I'm just a man who loves his wife and children. I'm not a psycho. I'm not mad. I couldn't go to jail. I've been away from you for two whole weeks and it almost killed me, Gail. I couldn't go to prison and be away from you for years.'

Gail tries to smile, to go along with what he's saying. 'I'd come to visit you.'

'The kids are in the car, we're all going away from here, It's all arranged.'

'Where are we going?' she asks.

'Miles away. No police, no press, no neighbours, we'll just go. But first I have to ask you to put your arms out in front of you. I'm really sorry Gail but I have to tie you up so you can't try to escape.'

Richard pulls out a roll of heavy-duty tape and uses it to tie Gail's wrists together. With her hands bound, he slips her wedding ring back onto her finger. Then he straightens his tie.

'Recognise the suit?'
'It's your wedding suit …' Gail says, confused.

Richard leads Gail into the garage where the car is parked. Sarah and David are inside the car, sitting together on the back seat. There's tape around their mouths and their wrists are taped together. Bethany lies asleep as Richard has given her a sedative.

'The truth is,' Richard tells Gail, 'If we can't live together as a family, then the only other option is for us to die together as a family.'

Gail begs, pleads with him as Sarah and David look on from the back seat of the car through the window.

'We can all live happily ever after,' Gail pleads. 'It's what I want, it's true!'
'I'm sorry but I'm going to have to gag you,' replies Richard.

Gail looks at the children in the car.

'Let me kiss them, a goodbye kiss, please, Richard.'

Richard opens the car door and Gail leans into the back seat to hold hands with Sarah and David.
'Everything's going to be alright,' she tells them.
As she holds Sarah's hand, Sarah opens her hand to show Gail a small pair of scissors she's holding.
'Everybody just relax now,' says Richard after he bundles Gail into the front seat of the car. 'Think about it as if it's a family holiday we're going on.'
He switches on the car stereo.

'I've brought us some music to listen to. Remember this one, Sarah? One of your favourites.'

Gail, David and Sarah are crying, sniveling, terrified. Richard starts up the car stereo and plays *The Wannadies 'You and Me'*.

Then he starts the car engine ... and tries to gas them inside the car in the locked garage.

As all of the chaos is happening inside the garage, Audrey is knocking at Gail's front door. She's come round for tea and can't understand why she can't get in the house until she works out that it's been bolted from inside. Over at Webster's garage, Kevin Webster and Tommy Harris are working and they come over, with Martin, to help Audrey find out what's wrong with the door.

Inside the garage, with the music still blaring, Richard ask Gail: 'Do you remember singing along to this one on our honeymoon in Florida? Singing our heads off, we were. It was the best three weeks of my life. And no one can ever take that away from us.'

In the back of the car, Sarah and David are working hard, quickly, using the scissors to cut through the tape around their wrists. Outside, Audrey can hear the music coming from the garage.

She tells Martin: 'There's somebody in the garage!'

Audrey, Martin, Tommy and Kevin huddle at the garage door and Audrey shouts: 'Gail? Gail? Is that you?'

Martin can hear a car engine running and looks at Audrey. They realise what's happening inside.

'It's him, Martin!' Audrey cries. 'He's back!'

The lads prise the garage door open and find Richard, Gail and the children in the car. The garage is full of exhaust fumes, everyone's coughing and crying. But now with the garage door open, Richard's plan to gas them has been foiled. Instead, he puts his foot down on the accelerator and speeds off out of the garage. Kevin, Tommy and Martin follow on in Tommy's car as fast as they can. Audrey heads to The Rovers to let everyone know what's happened and Archie gets her a very large brandy to calm her nerves.

'Ring the coppers, he's trying to kill them,' yells Tommy to Katy Harris, as he speeds off in pursuit of Richard's car.

In the back of Richard's car, David and Sarah finally manage to free their hands.
David leans forward into the front of the car, yelling: 'Richard! Stop the car! Stop the car!'

Richard ignores his pleas and keeps the car speeding through the dark streets. Then Sarah leans into the front of the car to cut Gail's hands free as David tries to pull the steering wheel from Richard's grasp. The car swerves dangerously all over the road, almost out of control.

With Gail's hands freed, both Gail and David try to pull the steering wheel to get Richard to stop the car - but Richard is determined not to be stopped.

'This IS IT!' he screams as he accelerates wildly.

Gail's eyes widen with horror when she sees where the car is heading - straight into the canal at 80 miles per hour.

'I LOVE YOU!' Richard screams as the car leaps off the canal-path and into the water.

As the car sinks below the murky surface of the canal, Gail, Sarah and David manage to pull themselves free, with little Bethany too.

Tommy and Martin help rescue them from the water just as the police and the fire brigade arrive.

And Richard?

He drowned in a watery grave, never to be seen again, bringing his reign of terror finally to an end.

It's over.

It's finally over.

Or is it…?

With Love, from Richard Hillman

It's now three years after Richard's death. When his funeral took place, Gail and undertaker Archie Shuttleworth were the only people to attend. Richard isn't a man who is missed or mourned by anyone. However, a permanent reminder remains on Coronation Street to the evil that was Richard Hillman. Outside the hair salon sits a memorial bench commemorating the life of Maxine Peacock.

But as life goes on for Gail and her family it appears that even years after his death, Richard Hillman is still able to control events in Gail's life, even from beyond the grave.

It starts on Sarah's birthday. She receives birthday cards from all of the family. There's one from Gail, one from David, one from Audrey, one from Bethany and one from Richard Hillman. *Hang on* ... Richard Hillman? Someone sends Sarah a card as if it's from Richard and she ends up in tears, hurt and angry that someone would do this to her as a joke. Gail quizzes David who swears he didn't send it.

The next card arrives on Valentine's Day. It's addressed to Gail and as she opens the envelope, her face drops.

'It's another one,' she says. 'Like Sarah's.' She reads out the wording inside. *'My heart is still yours.'*

It's addressed to Mrs. Gail Hillman.

'This is rubbish. Someone's idea of a joke. They can carry on. Send as many as they like. I'm not taking any notice. I'm not going to let Richard Hillman ruin my life. I won't even let him ruin Valentine's Day. He's not going to send another card.'

'He hasn't sent any. He's dead.' says Gail's new man, Phil Nail, concerned that Gail is becoming hysterical. Gail is clearly rattled by the arrival of the card. She rips it up and chucks it in the bin.

Gail receives a further card some days later. It's a condolence card which arrives on the anniversary of Richard's death. The message inside reads: *'I know you'll be thinking of me today. Together again soon! Love, Richard'*

Gail wonders who would be cruel enough to dig up the past like this?
Phil is working on an essay on his laptop when Gail opens the card. She hands it to Phil for him to see and while he studies it, Gail looks at his laptop with a worried expression on her face.

'You don't think I've got anything to do with all this, do you?' Phil asks.
'Why would I think that?
'I don't know. The way you were looking at my laptop...'
'It just reminded me of him. He used to work there all the time.'
'Well, who would know this is the anniversary of his death?'
'Anyone could find that out.' Gail replies.

'If the signature's as close to the real thing as you say it's ...'
'You don't think it could be the real thing, do you?'
'It's not a message from the other side.' Phil tells Gail sternly, as he fully believes that David is the one sending the mystery cards. 'It's a message from an attention-seeking teenager.'
'Why would David want to bring all this back up?' wonders Gail.

Gail speaks to David about the cards and he denies sending them. But he does reveal to his mum that he's still having nightmares about Richard driving them all into the canal. This is something that David had kept from Gail, she never knew that Richard's actions were still affecting David so much, after all these years.

'I was tied up, gagged, and driven into a canal. I still have nightmares about it now!'

Gail defends her son to Phil. 'He wouldn't do it, Phil. It's too raw.'
'Are you happy now you've got that out of me, are you?' David yells at Phil. ''Cos you're fascinated by all this, aren't you? You might just get another chapter for your never ending essay out of it.'
'Now come on, David ...' says Gail, but David won't let up.
'What's it called Phil? *The Haunting of Hillman*? *How families crack under pressure?*'

On Gail's birthday, there's yet another card signed by Richard Hillman. Gail's upset and in tears and close to a nervous breakdown.

She becomes paranoid and seriously starts thinking that Richard could still be alive, tormenting her. Audrey tells Gail to pull herself together and reminds Gail that she saw Richard's dead body when it was pulled out of the canal.

But Gail's paranoia and worry over the cards turn her demented. She even starts believing Eileen Grimshaw is evil enough to be the one sending the cards. She finally calls the police and puts the blame squarely, but wrongly, on Eileen.

There's an undercurrent of terror on the cobbles with the arrival of the cards as Richard Hillman's name is whispered once again on Coronation Street.

In The Rovers, the Duckworths recall how he swindled them out of their savings with a dodgy financial portillo, sorry, portfolio. And in the Kabin, Ashley and Fred grimly recall the night he killed Maxine.

So who could be sending the cards to Gail? Gail blames just about everyone she knows and wonders if Aidan Critchley could be behind the cruel joke.
The mystery deepens when Les Battersby tells Claire Peacock he picked up a fella in his taxi-cab who looks just like Richard Hillman. Could it be Richard's brother? His son? Or is it just a coincidence?

Gail stops going to work, she's too stressed to cope and starts taking sleeping pills to carry on. She's sick with the memories of Richard Hillman that have been thrown back into her life with the cards that someone is sending her. The whole thing is taking its toll and she starts having nightmares. She even thinks everyone on the street is talking about her.

Sadly for Gail, they are.

Gail continues to receive yet more cards but something spooky happens with one of them. It hasn't been posted, it just turns up on the kitchen table while David's off school, asleep in his bedroom upstairs. There's a red smudge on the back of the card, possibly blood, which puzzles Gail until David reveals he's got a paper cut on his finger. The pieces of the puzzle fall into place and Gail eventually suspects her own son of being the secret card sender.

Gail confides in Audrey that she believes David is the one responsible, but Audrey won't believe it of her grandson.

So, Gail searches his room and sure enough, she finds an unused greetings card. She sets a trap and lies to David that this Friday would have been Richard's birthday. She tells him that she's expecting another card in the post. On Friday, Gail sorts through the post.

Just as she breathes a sigh of relief to be proved wrong when there's no card there, Keith Harris knocks on her door with a card for her, it's been wrongly delivered to his house.

Gail knows then that she has to reveal her findings to David and she admits that she set him up. David doesn't even pretend, or lie. Immediately he confesses to Gail that it was him and that he thought that it was just a funny thing to do.

Just a funny thing to do?

Gail is furious with him, absolutely furious. She yells: 'I don't think you understand how much trouble you're in. You have set out - deliberately - to cause fear and misery to everyone in this family. This has been hanging over us for weeks... months...We've had sleepless nights. I'm on pills, for God's sake! The neighbours think I was sending these cards myself, that I'm mad. I thought I was going mad ... You know all this, you watched it all happen, and yet you carried on sending more cards. It's such a - sick - thing to do.'

David tries to hold back the tears that threaten to overwhelm him.

When Gail calms down, David tries to make amends by taking his mum a cup of tea, but she tells him that it will take a lot more than that to make up for his actions.

David blames the whole episode on his teenage angst and complains that no one listens or pays attention to him unless he does something wrong.

Little does Gail know that David's feelings about being ignored and craving attention will lead to his behaviour bringing back even worse memories of Richard Hillman into their lives.

You and Me, Always – Again

Life for David, it's fair to say, doesn't run smoothly. Gail knows how evil her son can be and she knows he has problems. But even Gail would never expect him to do what he does next.

David's evil behaviour over the years since Richard Hillman's death plunge into the canal forces Gail to throw him out of the family home. David's now living with his gran, who can barely tolerate the lad but knows she can't see her grandson homeless, however evil he might be.

When Gail's household is in full flow with wedding preparations for Sarah's wedding to Jason Grimshaw, David forces his family to pay attention to him - in a very dramatic way.

On Sarah and Jason's big day as the guests gather at the church, David drives his car to the canal, to the exact same spot where Richard Hillman tried to kill them so many years before. He parks the car canal-side and sits staring into the dark waters of the canal. From the car stereo, there's a song, a familiar song, playing.

It's *The Wannadies* singing *You and Me*, the very same song that Richard Hillman played when he tried to kill Gail, David, Sarah and Bethany by driving them all into the canal.

David revs his car engine and reverses up the bank away from the canal. He stops the car. Then, at full-speed, he drives his car back down the steep bank, and straight into the murky depths. The car sinks immediately. There's a man walking his dog along the canal who sees what's just happened and calls 999. The police and an ambulance arrive immediately and a police diver heads under the water.

At the church, just as Jason and Sarah are exchanging their vows, two police officers arrive. They break the news gently and quietly to Gail that David has driven his car into the canal.

Gail is in shock, but with Audrey and Bill Webster as support, she heads with the police to the canal. Gail stands open-mouthed with fear when she sees the spot where David has driven into the water.

'I knew it when we started heading this way!' she says.

'What? asks Bill, confused.

'This is where Richard Hillman brought them,' says Audrey.

'It's where he tried to… kill us,' sobs Gail.

David survives his death plunge. Gail and her family try to put the past behind them and move on with their lives.

With all the rotten luck they've had with Richard Hillman trying to kill them and then David's behaviour since then, surely it must be time for things to turn around? Surely things can only get better for Gail and her family?

All Gail needs to do now is just find the right man ... how hard can that be?

THE END

List of main characters in this story

Richard Hillman The best soap villain that Coronation Street's ever had; Norman Bates with a briefcase

Gail Platt / Hillman Married Richard, should have known better

Nick Tilsley Gail's eldest son from her marriage to Brian Tilsley

David Platt Gail's youngest son from her marriage to Martin Platt

Sarah Platt Gail's daughter from her marriage to Brian Tilsley

Bethany Platt Sarah's baby daughter, Gail's grand-daughter

Martin Platt Gail's ex-husband, father to David

Audrey Roberts Gail's mum, who Richard tried to kill

List of all other characters mentioned in this story

Aidan Critchley	Sarah's boyfriend, Richard framed him for Maxine's murder and for the attack on Emily
Alma Baldwin	Richard's cousin
Archie Shuttleworth	Undertaker, friend of Audrey
Ashley Peacock	Grieving widower, was married to Maxine
Blanche Hunt	Deirdre's acid-tongued mother
Candice Stowe	Sarah's best friend
Charlie Ramsden	Next door neighbour to Gail Platt. Teacher, alcoholic, married to Dr Matt Ramsden
Deirdre Barlow	Stalwart of the Street, married to Ken
Dev Alahan	Corner shop owner
Duggie Ferguson	Landlord of the Rovers Return. Died due to his dodgy dealings with Richard
Edna Miller	Cleaner at The Rovers Return. Predicted Duggie Ferguson's death

Eileen Grimshaw	Gail's enemy and mother of Todd and Jason
Emily Bishop	Richard tried to kill her for her life-savings and he bought her house.
Emma Watts	Curly's wife; policewoman
Fred Elliott	Maxine's father-in-law and local butcher, I say butcher
Geoffrey (Spider) Nugent	Emily's favourite nephew
Hayley Cropper	Alma's best friend. Married to Roy
Jack Duckworth	Swindled by Richard. Married to Vera
Janice Battersby	Loud-mouth busy-body. Married to Les
Jason Grimshaw	Sarah's husband, Gail's son-in-law.
Josh Peacock	Maxine and Ashley's baby
Katy Harris	Daughter of Tommy Harris
Ken Barlow	Aidan Critchley's teacher. Married to Deirdre
Kevin Webster	Garage mechanic.
Les Battersby	Loud-mouth good-for-nowt.

Linda Baldwin	Mike Baldwin's new, very young wife
Marion Hillman	Richard Hillman's first wife, deceased
Matt Ramsden	Next door neighbour to Gail Platt. Doctor, married to Charlie Ramsden
Maxine Peacock	Richard killed her. She should have stayed at the party
Mike Baldwin	Factory owner, local big-wig. Was married to Alma
Molly Hardcastle	Practice Nurse at Rosamund Street medical centre
Norman (Curly) Watts	Councillor. Married to Emma
Norris Cole	Busy-body who mistrusted Richard from the start. Richard kidnapped and threatened him
Patricia Hillman	Richard's second wife. He killed her
Phil Nail	Gail's boyfriend
Rita Sullivan	Goddess of Coronation Street
Roger Hinde	Richard's best man at his wedding to Gail

Roy Cropper	Local café owner, married to Hayley
Sally Webster	Gail's friend
Shelley Unwin	Barmaid at The Rovers Return
Steve McDonald	Local business owner, worked with Richard on renovating the flats
Todd Grimshaw	Candice's boyfriend, Jason's brother
Tommy Harris	Worked at the garage with Kevin. Dad to Katy.
Vera Duckworth	Swindled out of life savings by Richard Hillman. Married to Jack

About the Author

Glenda Young is a life-long Coronation Street fan. The show has been a part of her life as long as she can remember.

She's editor of Coronation Street fan websites, the Coronation Street Blog and Corrie.net.

<u>Glenda is author of the following:</u>

- Deirdre: A Life on Coronation Street
  Century Random House / ITV Publishing (2015)

- A Perfect Duet - the diary of Roy and Hayley Cropper. An unofficial Coronation Street companion book.
  FBS Publishing (2014)

- Coronation Street: The Complete Saga –
  Glenda updated this book with events from the cobbles from 2008-2010
  Carlton Publishing (2010)

- Coronation Street: The Novel
  Glenda updated this book with events from the cobbles from 2003-2008
  Carlton Publishing (2008)

Find out more at glendayoungbooks.com

Useful Websites:

Coronation Street Blog
http://coronationstreetupdates.blogspot.com
Twitter: @CoroStreetBlog
Facebook:
http://www.facebook.com/CoronationStreetBlog

Corrie.net
http://www.corrie.net

Cover artwork by Jo Blakeley
Website - **pickledjo.dunked.com/**
Twitter - **twitter.com/pickledjo**
Facebook - **www.facebook.com/Pickledjo**

Printed in Great Britain
by Amazon